ANIMALS ON THE EDGE
RHINO

ANIMALS
ON
THE EDGE
RHINO

by Anna Claybourne

BLOOMSBURY

LONDON BERLIN NEW YORK SYDNEY

Published 2012 by
Bloomsbury Publishing Plc
50 Bedford Square, London, WC1B 3DP

www.bloomsbury.com

ISBN HB 978-1-4081-4823-5
ISBN PB 978-1-4081-4956-0

Picture acknowledgements:
Cover: Shutterstock
Insides: All Shutterstock except for the following; p18, top © ZSL, bottom ©
ZSL, p19 © ZSL, p22 ©ZSL, p32 right ©Ed Schipul via Wikimedia Commons.

Manufactured and supplied under licence from the Zoological Society of London.

Produced for Bloomsbury Publishing Plc by Geoff Ward.

A CIP catalogue for this book is available from the British Library.

Printed in China by C&C Offset Printing Co.

CONTENTS

MEET THE RHINOCEROS

If you really did meet a rhinoceros, right now, you might be a bit nervous! The rhino is a BIG animal. The biggest ones, white rhinos, can grow up to 4m long, and 2m tall. They weigh as much as 50 men, and could fill your whole front room!

The rhino's nose

The name "rhinoceros" comes from ancient Greek, and simply means "nose-horn". You can easily tell rhinos from other creatures by the thick, pointed horns on their snouts. No other animal has anything quite like them. Rhinos are also known for their incredibly thick skin, and their heavy, chunky bodies.

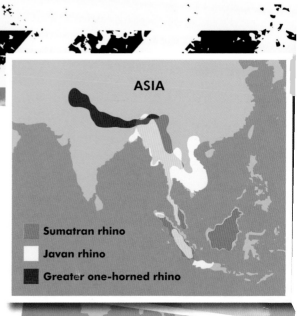

ASIA

- Sumatran rhino
- Javan rhino
- Greater one-horned rhino

AFRICA

- Black rhino
- White rhino

WHAT IS A RHINO HORN?

A rhino's horn isn't bony. It's actually made from a substance called **keratin**, which is also in bird's beaks, cows' hooves, and your hair and fingernails. Rhinos use their horns for digging in the ground, nudging babies along, and for fighting other rhinos or showing off to them. The rhino's horn is a big reason why people hunt it. The horns are used to make traditional medicines and knife handles.

ive rhinos

. long time ago, there used to be
ozens of different **species**, or types,
f rhinos. Today, most of them have
iied out. There are now just five rhino
pecies, living in parts of Africa and
sia. They are:

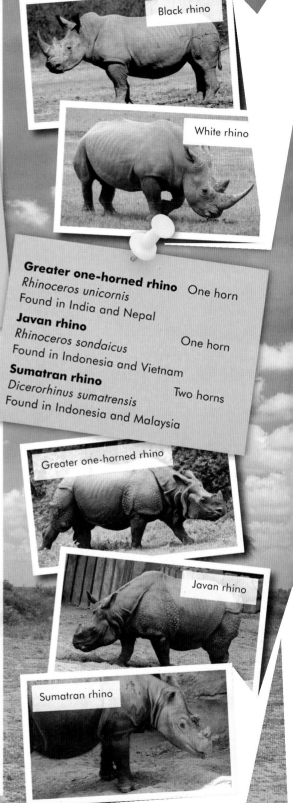

Black rhino

White rhino

Black rhino
Diceros bicornis
Found in southern and eastern Africa
Two horns

White rhino
Ceratotherium simum
Found in southern Africa
Two horns

Black rhinos and white rhinos are not
actually black and white – they're both grey!

Greater one-horned rhino
Rhinoceros unicornis
Found in India and Nepal
One horn

Javan rhino
Rhinoceros sondaicus
Found in Indonesia and Vietnam
One horn

Sumatran rhino
Dicerorhinus sumatrensis
Found in Indonesia and Malaysia
Two horns

The names in italics are the rhinos'
Latin names, which scientists use
to describe them. For example,
Rhinoceros unicornis (the greater one-
horned rhino's Latin name) means
"nose-horn with a single horn".

Greater one-horned rhino

Javan rhino

Sumatran rhino

Rhinos in danger

Today, there are only one-tenth
as many rhinos as there were 40
years ago. For a long time, people
have been hunting rhinos, and
destroying their **habitats** – the
natural surroundings they like to live
in. Three rhino species – black, Javan
and Sumatran rhinos – are now very
seriously **endangered**, and at risk
of dying out. In this book, as well as
reading all about rhinos, you can find
out about rhino **conservation** – the
things we are doing to try to help
them survive.

RHINOS ON THE EDGE

Rhinos are facing serious problems – and some species **really are on the edge of becoming extinct. If we don't help them, they could soon die out, and disappear for ever. But why has this happened?**

What are the problems?

These are the main reasons why rhinos are at risk:

- **Habitat loss** Wild rhino habitat is disappearing, as people cut down forests and take over wild land.
- **Hunting for horns** Buying and selling rhino horn is banned, but it still happens – so the hunting continues.
- **Bushmeat** Hunters also kill rhinos for bushmeat (wild animal meat).
- **Trophy hunting** In the past, people hunted a lot of rhinos just for sport.

RARE RHINOS

There were once millions of rhinos, but today, there are fewer than 30,000 living in the wild. Most of them are white rhinos. There are only about 270 Sumatran rhinos left, and just 60 of the rarest rhino of all, the Javan rhino.

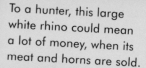

To a hunter, this large white rhino could mean a lot of money, when its meat and horns are sold.

Endangered species

How do we know when a species is endangered? The **IUCN** – the International Union for Conservation of Nature – gives each living species a **conservation status**, based on the situation it is in:

Black rhino: **Critically endangered** – at very high risk of dying out.
White rhino: **Near threatened** – could become endangered.
Greater one-horned rhino: **Vulnerable** – likely to become endangered.
Javan rhino: Critically endangered
Sumatran rhino: Critically endangered

There are about 1200 rhinos, like this greater one-horned rhino, living in captivity in zoos and wildlife parks around the world.

On the EDGE

The three most endangered rhinos are also listed as "**EDGE**" species by the EDGE of Existence programme. EDGE stands for Evolutionarily Distinct and Globally Endangered. **ZSL**, the Zoological Society of London, runs this conservation scheme to help animals that are not only rare and at risk, but also unusual, with few living relatives.

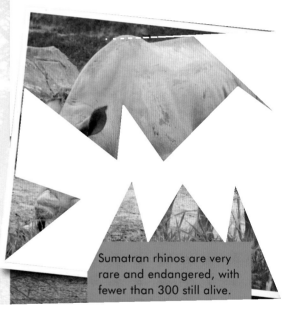

Sumatran rhinos are very rare and endangered, with fewer than 300 still alive.

EXTINCT GIANT

Indricotherium was a prehistoric animal closely related to today's rhinoceroses (though it didn't have a horn). It was HUGE – as big as a medium-sized dinosaur. It died out about 23 million years ago.

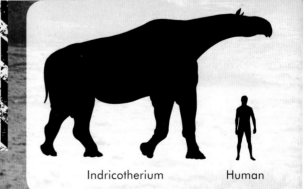

Indricotherium   Human

TALES OF THE RHINO

People have always been fascinated by the rhinoceros. Rumours and reports from long ago described it as a magical animal, a bizarre mixture of different beasts, or a ferocious mythical monster.

Mythical unicorns don't look much like rhinos – but stories about them could have grown from rhino sightings.

Strange beast

An ancient Roman writer, Pliny the Elder, told of a creature he called the "monoceros" – now thought to be a rhinoceros. He said:

"The most fierce and furious beast of all other, is the Licorne or Monoceros. His body resembles a horse, his head a stag, his feet an elephant, his tail a boar. He bellows in a hideous manner, and he has one black horn in the middle of his forehead, two cubits* in length. This wild beast cannot possibly be caught alive!"

*A cubit is about 45cm – so two cubits is nearly a metre.

However, at certain times, the Romans did actually catch live rhinos and other animals such as elephants. They brought them to Rome and made them fight each other as entertainment. Indian emperors used to do this too.

IS THIS THE UNICORN?

You may have noticed that the Greater one-horned rhino's Latin name, *Rhinoceros unicornis*, looks familiar. The unicorn – meaning "one horn" – is a mythical, magical creature, said to be a horse with a single, long horn on its forehead. The legend of the unicorn could have come from jumbled stories about the rhinoceros.

1515
RHINOCERVS

Dürer's famous picture was published with a description of the rhino, though it wasn't very accurate! It claimed: "It is the colour of a speckled tortoise, and is almost entirely covered with thick scales".

Dürer's rhinoceros

In 1515 Portuguese sailors visiting India brought back a gift of a live rhinoceros. At that time, many people in Europe still thought rhinos were just a myth. They were amazed to see one, and rumours about it spread fast. A German artist, Albrecht Dürer, made a famous woodcut artwork of the beast. He had never seen it himself – he just followed someone else's description.

BULLETPROOF SKIN

Another myth claims that the rhino's super-thick skin is bulletproof. This isn't actually true – hunters have shot many rhinoceroses dead. However, in the 1100s, Chinese warriors did wear armour made from rhinoceros skin.

On some parts of its body, a rhino's skin can be up to 4cm thick.

RHINOS AT HOME

Rhinos can survive in many habitats, depending on what species they are, and where in the world they live. But all their homes have one thing in common: there must be plenty of plants to eat!

Who lives where?

Africa's white and black rhinos like to live in patchy forests, or grasslands with lots of trees dotted around. Javan and Sumatran rhinos are smaller, and live in thick rainforests. And in India and Nepal, the greater one-horned rhino prefers to live in low-lying, swampy areas with thick, tall grass. This giant "elephant grass" can sometimes grow over 5m tall – as high as a house!

A greater one-horned rhino **forages** among grasses in its home in Nepal.

The dust flies as two male rhinos come face-to-face in a fierce fight.

FIGHT!

Male rhinos sometimes fight each other over territory. They bellow and roar, charge at each other, and swipe and slash with their horns. Greater one-horned rhinos use their teeth to fight instead, as their horn is short and stumpy. The loser is usually chased away, but some fights end up with one male being killed.

A crash or herd of white rhino females, or **cows**, and babies.

Rhino routine

Most rhinos are solitary, meaning they like to live alone. But white rhino females usually form a herd – also called a **crash** – of around 12 females and their **calves**.

On a typical day, a rhino spends several hours eating plants, especially in the morning and evening. In between meals, rhinos love to wallow in muddy pools and swamps. If they don't have a nice, damp hollow to wallow in, they will dig one in the ground, using their horns.

Wallowing in mud or water is relaxing for rhinos, and helps them cool down. Coating their skin with mud also helps to keep biting insects away.

CHAAAAARRGE!

When a rhino is annoyed, or wants to attack, it will charge towards its enemy at a scary speed. Though they're so bulky and chunky, rhinos can gallop along at almost 60 km/h – faster than the fastest human sprinters.

Get off my patch!

Male or **bull** rhinos mark out a **territory**, an area that they see as their own. They warn other males to stay away by leaving neat piles of poo around their territory. They also paw the ground to mark it with a special scent, which comes from **glands** in their feet. Females can enter a male's territory, though, so that males can mate with them.

RHINOS IN THE ZOO

Where's the nearest rhino to you right now? It's probably closer than you think, because a lot of zoos around the world keep rhinos. The rhinos you'll see in a zoo will probably be black, white, Sumatran, or greater one-horned rhinos. Very few Javan rhinos have ever been kept in zoos.

Who's in the zoo?

It can be tricky to keep white rhinos in zoos, because they like being in a herd – and a big herd of big rhinos is too much for most zoos! So white rhinos are only kept in very large zoos with lots of space.

A black rhino goes for a contented stroll around its zoo enclosure.

ENTERTAINMENT

Zoo rhinos usually have activities and toys to keep them busy. They can include:

- Logs or tyres dangling on ropes
- Balls with holes in them, to hide bits of food in
- Fruit-flavoured ice blocks
- Unbreakable balls for pushing around
- Different scents dotted around the enclosure
- Waterfalls and water sprays
- Sound recordings of other rhinos
- Wind chimes

Rhinos enjoy rubbing and scratching against fenceposts and walls.

A home from home

Zoos used to keep animals in small cages and yards. However, now that more research has been done about the needs of each animal, they try to make **enclosures** as big, comfortable and natural as possible. A typical rhino enclosure has:

- Lots of space to exercise, as rhinos like to run up and down
- A choice of different areas and surroundings to explore
- Natural habitat such as grass to nibble, and trees for shade
- Scratching posts and logs to rub against
- A muddy pool for wallowing in
- A heated indoor area, especially in cold countries.

Rhinos are used to warm weather in the wild. If it gets very cold, they may need to shelter.

Clara the rhinoceros was a big celebrity in the 1740s. This is one of the souvenir pictures of her sold by her owner, Douwe Mout van der Meer.

Rhino room-mates

A zoo might keep a rhino in an enclosure by itself, or put two or more females together for company. To let rhinos breed, they bring a male and a female together for a while. But because they might fight each other, the keepers have to be able to separate them quickly.

CLARA ON TOUR

Clara was a famous greater one-horned rhinoceros who lived in the 1700s. She was rescued from the wild as a baby after her mother was killed, and brought to the Netherlands. Her keepers took her all over Europe by ship and wooden carriage, showing her to the public.

RHINO FOOD

Like other large plant-eaters, rhinos need to eat... and eat... and eat! Grass and leaves don't contain very much energy, so rhinos have to gobble up massive amounts of them to keep going. A wild white rhino, for example, chomps its way through about 80kg of food every day – as much as an average man weighs.

In the wild

Wild rhinos aren't very fussy – they will eat all kinds of different plants and plant parts. White rhinos eat mainly grass, but the other species also eat leaves, stems, shoots, twigs, small branches, fruit and seeds. They have upper lips that can wrap around and grasp grass stalks and other food, and pull it into their mouths.

Finding food

Most rhinos live in places full of wild plants, so they don't have to go far to find food. They just wander around slowly, usually in the morning and evening, grazing and nibbling away. To munch the tasty tops of grasses that are too tall to reach, Indian rhinos walk over the grass, using their stomachs to flatten it onto the ground.

A rhino enjoys munching a delicious mouthful of grass.

In the zoo

In most zoos, rhinos eat a lot of hay (dried grass), as it's easy to transport and store. Keepers also give them vegetables like lettuce and carrots, as well as some bread, seeds and grains, and fruit as a treat. They may also have **herbivore pellets**, a cereal-based food designed for plant-eaters. The keepers spread the food around the enclosure, and hide it for the rhinos to find.

RHINO FOOD SHOPPING LIST

A typical zoo's shopping list for the rhinos could include:

Hay
Carrots
Lettuce
Apples
Herbivore pellets
Browse (leaves and twigs)

Alfalfa
Cabbage
Sweet potatoes
Bananas
Vitamins

A captive black rhino keeps the grass in its enclosure well-trimmed!

SALT LICK

A "salt lick" doesn't sound very nice, but it's an important part of a rhino's diet. Salt licks are areas where natural chemicals from underground are found close to the surface. Animals lick at them to get **vitamins** and minerals their bodies need. In zoos, some rhinos have artificial salt licks, or get their vitamins in their food instead.

A selection of fresh and dried plant food, ready for rhino feeding time.

A DAY IN THE LIFE: RHINO KEEPER

Mark Holden is a rhino keeper at ZSL Whipsnade Zoo, working with its large herd of white rhinos. He explains what it's like being up close to a rhino, and what a zookeeper has to do each day.

Mark in his zookeeping gear – rhino keeping can be chilly!

A day with the rhinos

8:00am The first thing the keepers do in the morning is pop their heads into the enclosure, and check that all the rhinos are OK. They are normally fast asleep on their straw beds, but they wake up once they notice us.

10.00am We then put some hay out in the paddocks (outdoor areas) to encourage the rhinos to go outside. The rhinos walk out through a special rhino gate. As they go through it, the keepers can do a few quick medical checks, and weigh the rhinos too. We also do a bit of rhino training, teaching the rhinos to obey simple instructions. They are safer to work with if they'll do what we say!

The zoo needs a large supply of hay and straw to keep its rhinos happy.

12.00pm Once the rhinos are outside, it's time to clean their indoor enclosure. We clear out the dung and old hay, and wash the floors.

4.00pm After spending all day mooching around and grazing in their paddocks, the rhinos are called in for their dinner. They spend some time eating before settling down for the night.

DO RHINOS BITE?

The rhinos don't tend to bite the keepers, but they do have very strong lips and can give you a nasty suck!

Fun with the rhinos

Rhinos are quite touchy-feely animals, and you can build up a good relationship with them. They love having their ears tickled, and the soft bits under their front legs too – their "armpits". They enjoy it so much that sometimes they fall asleep whilst being tickled.

In the winter, the rhinos are sometimes less willing to go outside, so the keepers will build them snowmen! This gives them something new and interesting to push over and play with.

SNEAKY SNACK!

Rhinos love eating. One of the older females once found a door leading to the store cupboard, pushed it open, and munched her way through lots of food before she was found!

Mark would like to say hi to male rhino Sizzle, but he's too busy munching!

RHINO BABIES

Rhinos are huge, and their babies are pretty big too. But a rhino baby, or calf, can be attacked by predators like lions and crocodiles, or even by male rhinos. It has to keep close to its mum to stay safe.

Meeting up

Most rhinos live alone, or in female-only groups. But to mate and have babies, a male and a female need to get together. A female shows she is looking for a mate by spreading urine around a male's territory. The male follows her, and charges towards her or swings his head at her, before running away. After doing this for a while, the pair can mate.

A male and female black rhino mating. The female may become pregnant, and have a baby.

BORN WITH NO HORN

Rhino calves don't have any horns when they are born. It takes a few weeks for the horn to start to take shape.

You can see how long this mother white rhino's horn is, compared to her baby's tiny, stumpy horn.

Sometimes, rhinos in zoos abandon their calves. Keepers feed them milk from a bottle instead.

Having a baby

A baby rhino grows inside its mother for a **gestation period** of about 16 months. When it's born, it can weigh up to 80kg, and looks a bit like a pig. At first, the calf is weak and wobbly, but after about an hour, it can stand up. By three days old, it can run along with its mum. As rhinos are **mammals**, the baby feeds on milk from its mother's body at first. It stays with her until she has her next baby, usually around three years later.

Zoo babies

Some rhinos seem to have trouble breeding in zoos, but they have been more successful recently. Behin, a female greater one-horned rhino at ZSL's Whipsnade zoo, has had two calves: Asha, born in 2006, and Ajang, born in 2010. Ajang's name means "enormous" in Nepalese, as he was a very big baby!

A young rhino calf always stays close to its mother, eating, sleeping and moving around with her.

FACT FILE: GROWING UP

Weight at birth: 30-80 kg, depending on species.

Birth to 3-4 weeks: Feeds on mother's milk.

3-4 weeks: Begins eating grass or other plants.

18 months-2 years: Stops feeding on milk.

6 years (female) 10 years (male): Young rhinos become adults and can have their own babies.

Rhino lifespan: 30-50 years, depending on species.

ONE RHINO'S STORY: NSISWA

This is Nsiswa, nicknamed Sizzle - a white rhino living at ZSL Whipsnade Zoo, England. At Whipsnade, the white rhinos live as naturally as possible. They form a large herd and can roam around a very big, natural enclosure. Sizzle is the herd's dominant male, or bull.

Born in Africa

Sizzle was born in South Africa, on a wildlife reserve. At one stage, the reserve had only 30 rhinos living in it, as a result of hunting. But thanks to successful protection, the numbers of rhinos went up and up. Eventually, it was too full, and some of the rhinos needed new homes. So Nsiswa was brought to live at Whipsnade Zoo in 1991, in the hope that he would make a good breeding bull.

BULLS IN THE ZOO

White rhinos are happiest in zoos if they can live in a large group – but there must be only one dominant male, like Sizzle. If the keepers put two big bulls together, they would probably fight.

Sizzle needs to eat a lot of the time, as he's big and energetic.

Big Daddy

Sizzle happily took on the role of dominant male in the herd. Mating with the herd's females, he has become father to an amazing twelve new calves. It can be hard to breed white rhinos in zoos, but Whipsnade's extra large enclosure and natural-sized herd seem to help. Thanks to this – and to Sizzle! – Whipsnade now has the most successful white rhino breeding programme in Europe.

What's Sizzle like?

Sizzle is a big, bulky rhino, a typical dominant male. But he's friendly, too. He will often wait indoors in the morning for the keepers to come and give him a good scratch. When it rains, or when he wallows in the mud, Sizzle can go a bit crazy. He leaps around and sprays mud everywhere – often all over the keepers!

This is one of the female rhinos that share the white rhino enclosure with Sizzle.

The rhinos at Whipsnade enjoy a lush, spacious outdoor living area.

NSISWA'S NAME

He's mainly known by his nickname, but Sizzle's real name, Nsiswa, was given to him in Africa.

THREATS TO RHINOS

On these pages you can find out a bit more about how rhinos have become endangered, and the dangers they still face.

Poaching

Poaching means hunting when it is against the law. Poachers try to find and kill rhinos for their horns, even though they aren't supposed to. So why do they do it? The reason is that they can make a lot of money selling the horns. Many people in China, Vietnam and some other countries believe that rhino horn is a powerful medicine that can cure all kinds of illnesses. Others, especially in a country called Yemen, buy rhino horn to make special dagger handles.

Bushmeat

Bushmeat is meat from wild animals. When people are very poor, you can understand why they go hunting for meat. A big animal like a rhino provides a lot of meat, so the hunters can eat some themselves and sell the rest. People have always hunted wild animals to eat, and it wasn't always a problem. But when those animals are endangered, and there aren't many of them left, it can be a disaster.

Some rhino poachers have hi-tech equipment such as helicopters. They swoop down quickly, shoot some rhinos, cut off their horns and escape in minutes.

Trophy hunting

People used to go hunting for big wild animals as a sport. Rhinos were one of the "big five" they wanted to shoot most, along with lions, leopards, buffaloes and elephants. A lot of rhinos died this way, and some still do.

Habitat loss

There are a lot of humans on Earth, and we take up a lot of space. Everywhere people live, they take wild land and turn it into roads, towns, and farmland. This takes natural habitat such as rainforest away from wild animals, and fewer of them can survive. Often, some wild habitat is left, but it's split up into small areas that are not connected to each other. This is called **habitat fragmentation**.

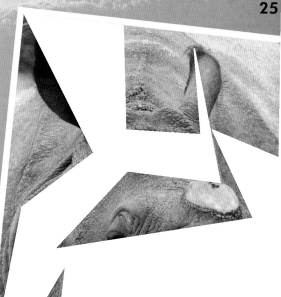

Some wildlife parks have tried removing rhino's horns safely, to save them from poachers. But it is hard to do, and doesn't always work, as poachers still kill them for other reasons.

IN THE LAB

Scientists from ZSL, the Zoological Society of London, have done tests on rhino horn to see if it really works as a medicine. It doesn't! They found that taking rhino horn is no better at curing illnesses than chewing your own fingernails.

It's better and more natural for rhinos to keep their horns if possible.

HELPING RHINOS

Sadly, humans have done a lot to harm rhinos. But there are some things we can do to help them now. These things work best when we do them all together. We need to solve all the problems facing rhinos, not just fix them one at a time.

A safe home

Rhinos need somewhere safe to live in the wild. Some of their habitat has been made into **wildlife sanctuaries** and **national parks**, where no one is allowed to build or farm. Some have fences around them, and some have **wardens** to patrol them and guard the wildlife.

Watching out for rhinos

Scientists and conservation workers carefully **monitor**, or keep track of, wild rhinos. They count them, and check how healthy they are, and how many babies they are having. Sometimes, they move rhinos around, to help them survive in the best possible habitat, with the right mixture of males and females so that they can breed.

White rhinos in Lake Nakuru National Park in Kenya, enjoying a perfect habitat with wide open spaces and muddy pools.

Ecotourism

At many national parks, tourists can go on safari to see amazing wildlife, such as rhinos, elephants, lions and tigers. They pay to visit, and this raises money for conservation.

Working in wildlife

Protecting rhinos takes a lot of work – and local people can get jobs doing that work. They can become wardens or park rangers in national parks, or wildlife **trackers** helping scientists to monitor rhinos. Ecotourism creates lots of jobs too, working in hotels or as tourist guides. This helps people make a living in new ways, instead of poaching or cutting down forests.

Tourists take an elephant ride to watch greater one-horned rhinos in Chitwan National Park, Nepal.

A simple sign like this can sometimes help to protect wild animals from danger.

In the zoo

Rhinos in zoos help us learn more about them, which makes it easier to help them in the wild. Zoos also raise money for conservation, by charging visitors to see the animals. Some also breed rhinos, helping to keep their numbers up.

Spreading the message

It's also important to let everyone know about endangered species. Special lessons in schools can help people learn why animals like rhinos are in danger. So can zoos, and books like this one!

NEPAL: THE GREATER ONE-HORNED RHINO

ZSL, the Zoological Society of London, is helping rhinos in two main areas: Kenya, where they work with black rhinos; and Nepal, home of the greater one-horned rhino.

There are now thought to be about 2,500 greater one-horned rhinos living in the wild, in just a few areas of India and Nepal.

The rare one-horned rhino

For thousands of years, India and Nepal, where one-horned rhinos live, have been home to lots of people. Over time, they've taken more and more land for farming and building on. Now, there are just a few small protected areas where the greater one-horned rhino can survive. Along with ZSL, the government of Nepal is working very hard to protect them – but the poachers are still trying to hunt them.

Bardia National Park

Chitwan National Park

Nepal

INDIA

Greater one-horned rhino

Chitwan and Bardia

Chitwan is Nepal's oldest national park. It's famous for its amazing wildlife – besides greater one-horned rhinos, there are Asian elephants, sloth bears, Bengal tigers and many other endangered and unique species.

Bardia National Park is a larger, very wild and remote park, with a mixture of grasslands and jungles criss-crossed with rivers. It's perfect for rhinos, but thanks to poaching in the past, only has about 35 of them.

Stopping the poachers

To try to keep poachers away, Nepal's national parks have specially trained anti-poaching teams to patrol the parks, checking for poachers. They can arrest any poachers they find. Soldiers armed with guns also patrol the parks, and the teams can call on them for help. Nepal has made its anti-poaching laws much stronger too, so once poachers are caught, they can be sent to prison for 10-15 years.

Does it work?

Poachers do still manage to kill rhinos in Chitwan, though they often get caught. But in Bardia, poaching has been almost completely banished. Number of rhinos are finally rising in both parks. Sometimes, conservation workers move rhinos from Chitwan to Bardia, where they are safer.

A wild greater one-horned rhino shelters among the long grasses and swampy pools of Chitwan National Park.

These tourists at Chitwan are going wildlife-watching from a boat, which lets them get close to animals quietly.

FIGHTS IN THE FOREST

When anti-poaching teams come face-to-face with poachers, things can get dangerous. Poachers will do anything they can to escape. If the teams have armed guards to help them, it can sometimes turn into a battle. You have to be pretty brave to be in an anti-poaching patrol.

A DAY IN THE LIFE: RHINO WARDEN

Wildlife wardens **work in national parks, monitoring wildlife and helping to run the park. In Nepal's national parks, rhino wardens have plenty to do. They follow the rhinos, count them, check their health, report any problems, and help the tourists who visit the parks.**

Riding high

Nepal's greater one-horned rhinos live mainly in floodplains – areas that are often flooded. They are a mixture of forests, rivers and very, very tall grasses. To see over the high grass, the wardens often ride elephants! The elephants are well-trained and fairly tame. Each elephant has a trainer, or **mahout**, who comes along to look after it.

Elephants can easily cross most rivers and ponds, making them a great way to get around in Chitwan.

In the jungle

The rhino's jungle habitat isn't always very pleasant for people! It's very hot and humid, meaning the air is damp and you sweat a lot. In May and June, the temperature can reach a sweltering 40°C. The tall grasses where the rhinos live can be very sharp, and cut your skin. On top of that, there are dangerous animals around. Rhinos themselves can charge and trample you, and there are also wild elephants, tigers, leopards and deadly snakes such as cobras.

JUNGLE GEAR

When trekking in the forests, wardens take with them:

Camouflaged, lightweight clothing
Long sleeves and trousers to protect against grass and biting insects
Water bottle
Binoculars
Forms to fill in with notes and measurements
Camera
GPS (Global Positioning System) that shows where they are.

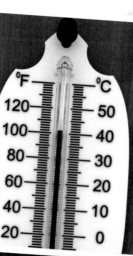

40°C is hotter than human body temperature. In the steamy, humid jungle, it's a bit like being in a hot bath!

AT HOME IN A HUT

While working in the national parks, the wardens live in small base camps with a few wooden huts. The huts are on stilts, so that when the **monsoon** rains come and flood the land, they stay dry. They don't have fridges, so the wardens eat food that keeps well and doesn't go off – mainly rice, chapattis and lentils. They contain lots of energy and protein to keep the wardens going on their jungle patrols.

A greater one-horned rhino wanders close to a pathway in Kaziranga National Park, India.

KENYA: THE BLACK RHINO

Kenya, in East Africa, was once home to many thousands of black rhinos. But in the 1970s, rhino horn poaching went crazy. It got so bad, three rhinos were being killed every day. By 1990, Kenya only had a few hundred black rhinos left.

Time to act!

In 1990, Kenya's government set up the Kenya Wildlife Service to help wildlife. Black rhinos were moved to sanctuaries with fences around them, to keep poachers out. Some farms also helped by keeping rhinos on their private land. And tough new laws meant armed rangers could defend wildlife from poachers. It worked – the rhino **population** started to grow again.

The famous Kenyan scientist Richard Leakey was the first boss of the Kenya Wildlife Service. He helped raise money for it from around the world.

This map shows the location of Kenya's Tsavo East National Park, where rhinos are being carefully monitored.

KENYA

Tsavo East National Park

THE ROLE OF RHINOS

Saving rhinos actually helps to protect their whole **ecosystem** – their natural habitat and the living things in it. As rhinos munch at plants, they open up space so that smaller animals like antelopes can find food. When rhinos eat fruit, the seeds come out in their poo. This helps plants to spread their seeds around and grow in lots of places.

Moving black rhinos can be dangerous, as they are known for being quite grumpy and **aggressive**.

MOVING A RHINO

Moving a rhino is a big job! First, it is shot with a **tranquilizer dart**, sometimes from a helicopter, to make it sleep. Then, a big team of people help to move it into a crate. Sometimes, elephants are used to pull the crate to a truck for transporting the rhino. In Africa, they sometimes use helicopters to airlift the rhinos instead.

Working together

In the 1990s, ZSL began to help with Kenya's black rhino project. It brought in extra money, and ZSL scientists trained more people to work with the rhinos. Over time, the sanctuaries filled up. Finally, in 2008, Kenya began to release black rhinos back into the wild – in Tsavo East National Park, where 7,000 rhinos once lived.

600... and counting

From a low point of about 350, the number of black rhinos in Kenya has risen to over 600. The aim is to have 1000 living there by 2020, and eventually, 2000. But poachers are still a problem, so it's a constant struggle to protect the rhinos.

A tranquilizer dart injects the rhino with a drug that makes it go to sleep for a while, but doesn't harm it.

MANAGING RHINOS

Managing **rhinos means looking after them very carefully, watching them closely, and setting up their surroundings to help them survive. ZSL conservation workers manage rhinos like this in both Kenya and Nepal. So how does it work?**

Spotting problems

Careful checking allows wardens to spot problems and fix them fast. They can:

- Find out when rhinos are ill, and get them treated by a vet.
- Track down an individual rhino that's causing problems, and move it.
- Rescue baby rhinos that have lost their mothers, for example because of poaching.
- Find out when an area is getting too crowded, and move some of the rhinos somewhere else.

Habitat checking

Before moving rhinos around, or releasing them into a new area, conservationists have to be sure they will have everything they need. So they monitor the habitat, too. They check what types of plants and trees are there, and how many rhinos they can feed. They make sure there are not too many other big animals, like elephants, that could eat the rhinos' food or fall out with them.

Wild animals have more babies when they are happy and relaxed. If they are stressed, the birth rate goes down.

Baby count

Left to breed on their own, a group of wild rhinos can grow in number by 8% each year. That means if there are 100 rhinos this year, there could be 108 next year.

Careful rhino management can improve on that. Wardens check how many females there are, and how many babies they have – and try to give them the best conditions for breeding. This way, the growth rate can reach 11% – 100 rhinos could become 111 rhinos in a year.

BEWARE OF THE RHINO!

Working closely with rhinos, especially black rhinos, can be risky. They are huge and heavy, and can charge at people if they are annoyed. Rhinos can't see very well, but they do have a good sense of smell and hearing. They know if someone is nearby, but they can't tell what's happening or if they're in danger. So they charge, just to be sure!

When rhinos charge, they often "bluff", or stop just before they reach you – but you never know whether they will or not.

GETTING ON WITH RHINOS

For people who live close to them, wild rhinos can be a bit of a headache. They might be exciting to watch in the zoo – but not so much when they trample all over your precious crops, and munch them to shreds. They can also be dangerous to humans. So there are lots of schemes to help people and rhinos live happily side by side.

Buffer zones

Wild rhinos mainly live in sanctuaries, national parks or other protected areas. But these often lie alongside farmland. Only small sanctuaries have fences – in bigger parks, rhinos can wander off into fields and villages.

To deal with this, Nepal's national parks have **buffer zones** – strips of land around the park. In the buffer zones, there are extra patrols to watch out for rogue rhinos, and schemes to help local farmers. These are some of the things that can make life easier for them:

- Electric fences around their fields
- Ideas for new crops that rhinos don't like, such as chillies or menthol
- Jobs for local people in the parks, to give them a good income.
- Schemes to track down troublesome rhinos and move them to other areas.

These rhinos are being kept safely in an enclosure, so they can't wander out.

A strong, high fence or electric fence can protect crops from big wild animals.

Spreading the word

Some conservation workers don't work with the animals themselves – instead they work as education officers. They go into schools to tell children about rhinos and other endangered species – or bring school groups to the parks to show them around. They explain how keeping forests wild, and endangered species alive, can bring in money from tourists – but if they are all destroyed, that can't happen.

An education worker visits a school in Nepal.

FREE GAS

One scheme in the buffer zones in Nepal uses human and animal poo to make a kind of gas. People can use it for cooking, instead of taking firewood from the forest.

A village close to the buffer zone around Chitwan National Park.

PUTTING ON A PLAY

As another way to explain conservation to people around the park, conservation charities helped a local actor, Salil Kanika, to create a play about how rhino poaching works, called "Gaida – The Muddy Truth". (Gaida means rhino.) Some local people themselves played parts in the show, while others came to watch.

CONSERVATION BREEDING

Conservation breeding **means helping animals to breed in zoos or wildlife parks – that is, in** captivity. **Conservation breeding helps endangered species by keeping some of them alive, healthy and safe in zoos around the world. Animal babies are also super-popular. They appear in the news and bring more visitors to the zoo, raising extra money for conservation.**

Does it work for rhinos?

Not all rhino species breed well in captivity. White rhinos have fewer babies, perhaps because most zoos cannot recreate the lifestyle they have in the wild, living in very large open spaces. But black, Sumatran and greater one-horned rhino births are becoming more common in zoos, as vets and keepers find better ways to help them breed.

The baby book

Zoos that keep rhinos work together to keep a special book, called a **studbook**, for each species. It's a list of all the rhinos born in captivity, who their parents were, and their ages. This helps zoos plan which animals to bring together to mate. They move rhinos around from one zoo to another, to put rhinos into the best pairs or groups for breeding.

A white rhino baby takes a walk on its own.

A mother greater one-horned rhinoceros with her calf at Berlin Zoo, in Germany.

Asani and Bashira

As part of the European Endangered Species Breeding Programme, Chester Zoo in England breeds black rhinos. In 2008 and 2009, two new calves were born just 8 months apart, to two different mums. Baby boy Asani came first, born to Kitani and Sammy. The following year, a rhino pair named Ema and Magadi had a girl calf, Bashira.

GOING BACK

If an endangered species breeds really well in captivity, some animals can then be re-introduced, or released into the wild. This could be a good way to help rhinos in the future. The first **re-introduced** black rhinos are already surviving in the wild in South Africa.

TEST-TUBE BABIES

When rhinos mate, a male's sperm cell joins a female's egg cell, and they grow into a baby inside her body. It is possible for zoos to help a female rhino get pregnant without mating. They collect the sperm and egg cells from the male and female, and join them in a test tube. They then put the tiny rhino **embryo** inside the female to grow. This avoids having to move big, heavy rhinos around.

Test-tube breeding can improve the rate of rhino births in zoos.

CAN WE SAVE THE RHINO?

A lot of people are working incredibly hard to save the rhino.
But will it work? Could rhinos soon become extinct?

Fast fall

Rhinos are a scary example of just how quickly, and how far, a wild animal's population can fall. From hundreds of thousands of rhinos, most of the five species have plummeted to just a few handfuls here and there. When something is worth money, like the rhino's horn, there will always be someone who's prepared to steal it.

When they are protected from hunters, rhinos can live happily, and breed more easily.

Success stories

However, in some places, rhino conservation has worked well. Some endangered species never manage to start growing in number again. But greater one-horned rhinos and black rhinos are managing to do that, even if it's only slowly. And in Bardia National Park in Nepal, poaching has been completely stopped. No one knows how long that will last – but it shows that it is possible. If we keep trying, maybe the rhinos will be able to recover.

In the future, many more rhinos should be able to live safely in the wild, like these ones in Africa.

A CAREER IN CONSERVATION

If you love wild animals, you could become a zookeeper, a wildlife vet, or a conservation worker, scientist or park warden working in the wild. Choose science subjects, especially biology, to help you get there.

Being a national park warden is an exciting, skilled job that lets you work outdoors.

What can you do?

- **Go to the zoo** Visiting the zoo is a great day trip. Your entrance fee pays for animal care and conservation, and you get to see all kinds of amazing animals.
- **Adopt a rhino** Zoos and wildlife charities run animal adoption schemes, which are easy to join. You pay to adopt a rhino, and get updates on its progress.
- **Go wildlife watching** One day you might be able to go on a safari holiday to a national park. Or, if you're in the area, visit a national park or wildlife reserve for a day.
- **Don't help the rhino trade** Don't believe rhino horn could work as a medicine – it can't. Avoid buying traditional medicines, as several of them contain endangered animal parts.

ABOUT ZSL

The Zoological Society of London (ZSL) is a charity that provides conservation support for animals both in the UK and worldwide. We also run ZSL London Zoo and ZSL Whipsnade Zoo.

Our work in the wild extends to Africa and Nepal, where our conservationists and scientists are working to protect rhinos from extinction. These incredible animals are part of ZSL's EDGE of Existence programme, which is specially designed to focus on genetically distinct animals that are struggling for survival.

By buying this book, you have helped us raise money to continue our conservation work with rhinos and other animals in need of protection. Thank you.

To find out more about ZSL and how you can become further involved with our work visit **zsl.org** and **zsl.org/edge**

Young rhinos need their mums to be protected from poachers.

LIVING CONSERVATION

EDGE

ZSL LONDON ZOO

ZSL WHIPSNADE ZOO

Websites

Black rhino at EDGE of Existence
www.zsl.org/edgeblackrhino
Javan rhino at EDGE of Existence
www.zsl.org/edgejavanrhino
Sumatran rhino at EDGE of Existence
www.zsl.org/edgesumatranrhino
Rhinos of Nepal at Whipsnade Zoo
www.zsl.org/whipsnaderhinos

Places to visit

ZSL Whipsnade Zoo
Dunstable, Bedfordshire, LU6 2LF, UK
www.zsl.org/whipsnade
0844 225 1826

Many rhinos live in captivity, but there isn't enough space there for all of them.

Rhinos, like other wild animals, deserve a safe

GLOSSARY

aggressive Easily annoyed or violent.

breed Mate and have babies.

browse Leafy branches used as food for animals.

buffer zone A border area around a national park.

bull A male rhino.

bushmeat Meat that comes from wild animals.

calf A baby rhino.

captive breeding Breeding animals in zoos.

captivity Being kept in a zoo, wildlife park or garden.

census A population count.

conservation Protecting nature and wildlife.

conservation status How endangered a living thing is.

cow A female rhino.

crash A name for a group of rhinos.

critically endangered Very seriously endangered and at risk of extinction.

ecosystem A habitat and the living things that are found in it.

ecotourism Visiting wild places as a tourist to see wildlife.

EDGE Short for Evolutionarily Distinct and Globally Endangered.

embryo Cluster of cells that can grow into a living thing.

enclosure A secure pen, cage or other home or for a zoo animal.

endangered At risk of dying out and become extinct.

extinct No longer existing.

forage To search around for food.

gestation period Length of time a baby grows inside its mother.

gland Small organ that releases a body substance.

GPS Short for Global Positioning System, a way of finding where you are.

graze To nibble constantly at food.

habitat The natural surroundings that a species lives in.

habitat loss Damaging or destroying habitat.

habitat fragmentation Breaking up natural habitat into small areas.

herbivore A plant-eating animal.

herbivore pellets Special food for pet or zoo herbivores, or plant-eaters.

IUCN Short for the International Union for Conservation of Nature.

keratin Hoof-like substance that rhino horns are made of.

mahout Someone who looks after and trains an elephant.

mammal A kind of animal that feeds its babies on milk from its body.

manage To look after something, monitor it and carefully control it.

monitor To check, measure or keep track of something.

monsoon A seasonal wind that brings heavy rain and floods.

national park A protected area of land where wildlife can live safely.

near threatened May become endangered.

park ranger Someone who patrols and guards a national park.

poaching Hunting animals that are protected by law and shouldn't be hunted.

population Number of people, or animals, in a particular place.

predator An animal that hunts and eats other animals.

range The area where an animal or species lives.

re-introduce To release a species back into the wild.

shoot The first growth of a plant from a seed.

species A particular type of living thing.

studbook A record of the animals of a particular species born in captivity.

territory An area that an animal considers its own.

tracking Finding or following wild animals by their signs and marks.

tranquilizer dart A dart used to shoot an animal to make it fall asleep.

trophy hunting Hunting big animals for sport or to show off.

ultrasound scan A way of using sound waves to look inside the body.

vitamins Chemicals that your body needs, found in some foods.

vulnerable At risk, but not as seriously as an endangered species.

warden National park worker who looks after wildlife.

wildlife reserve A protected area of land where wildlife can live safely.

wildlife sanctuary An enclosed area where wildlife can live safely.

ZSL Short for Zoological Society of London.

FIND OUT MORE

Books

100 Things You Should Know About Endangered Animals by Belinda Gallagher, Miles Kelly Publishing, 2009

What's it Like to be a... Zoo Keeper? by Elizabeth Dowen and Lisa Thompson, 2010

Save the Black Rhino by Louise Spilsbury and Richard Spilsbury, Heinemann, 2007

Emi and the Rhino Scientist by Mary Kay Carson, Houghton Mifflin Harcourt, 2010

Nature Watch: Rhinos by Sally M. Walker, Lerner, 2007

Websites

Black rhinoceros at Brookfield Zoo
www.brookfieldzoo.org/czs/Brookfield/Exhibit-and-Animal-Guide/Pachyderm-House/Black-Rhinoceros

Black rhino at Chester Zoo
www.chesterzoo.org/animals/mammals/horses-and-rhinos/black-rhino

Rhino webcams at Paignton Zoo
www.paigntonzoo.org.uk/rhinocam.php

Chitwan National Park
www.chitwannationalpark.gov.np/

Places to visit

Paignton Zoo Environmental Park
Totnes Road, Paignton, Devon
TQ4 7EU, UK
www.paigntonzoo.org.uk

Edinburgh Zoo
Corstorphine, Edinburgh,
EH12 6TS, UK
www.edinburghzoo.org.uk/
0131 334 9171

Chester Zoo
Upton-by-Chester, Chester
CH2 1LH, UK
www.chesterzoo.org
01244 380280

Brookfield Zoo
8400 31st Street, Brookfield,
IL 60513, Chicago, USA
www.brookfieldzoo.org

San Diego Zoo
2920 Zoo Drive, Balboa Park,
San Diego, California, USA
www.sandiegozoo.org

INDEX

OTHER TITLES IN THE ANIMALS ON THE EDGE SERIES

www.storiesfromthezoo.com

Penguin
ISBN: HB 978-1-4081-4822-8
PB 978-1-4081-4960-7

Tiger
ISBN: HB 978-1-4081-4824-2
PB 978-1-4081-4957-7

Gorilla
ISBN: HB 978-1-4081-4825-9
PB 978-1-4081-4959-1

Hippo
ISBN: HB 978-1-4081-4826-6
PB 978-1-4081-4961-4

Elephant
ISBN: HB 978-1-4081-4827-3
PB 978-1-4081-4958-4